Molly Mischief

When I Grow Up

First published in the United Kingdom in 2018 by
Pavilion Children's Books
43 Great Ormond Street
London
WC1N 3HZ

An imprint of Pavilion Books Limited

Publisher and Editor: Neil Dunnicliffe
Art Director and Designer: Lee-May Lim

ISBN: 9781843653592

A CIP catalogue record for this book is available from the British Library.

10 9 8 7 6 5 4 3 2 1

Reproduction by Mission, Hong Kong
Printed by

This book can be ordered directly from the publisher online
at www.pavilionbooks.com, or try your local bookshop.

Molly Mischief

When I Grow Up

Adam Hargreaves

PAVILION

Hello, my name is **Molly**.

Some people call me **Molly Mischief** – I can't think why!

My mum and dad are always telling me what to do.

It's always **time** to do something.

Time for school.

MOLLY!

And time to go to bed. Much too early!

MOLLY!

I can't wait until I grow up.
Then Mum and Dad won't
be able to tell me what to do.

When I grow up I'll be able to do anything I like.
But what job will I do?

Maybe when I grow up I could be an **astronaut.**

Then again, maybe being an astronaut is not such a good idea.

Perhaps I could be a firefighter.

I tried being a firefighter. It was fun...

...and bake the best cakes
in the world.

I could be a scientist...

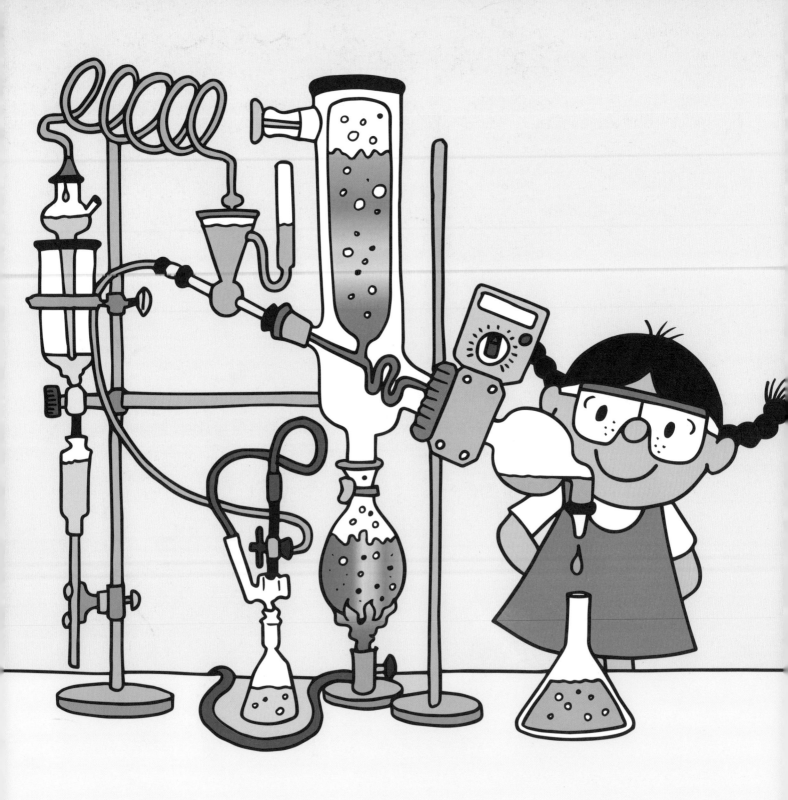

...and invent an amazing new invention.

I could be a deep sea diver
when I grow up.

I'm good at making people laugh.

Except for Dad!

MOLLY!

I really like reading.
I could be a librarian.

But maybe I'm too loud.

Then I had a thought.
If I had a job I wouldn't have time to play with my friends.

I wouldn't have time
to build treehouses.

I wouldn't have time to paint pictures.

I wouldn't even have time to tease my brother!

Do you know what?

I don't want to grow up.

Not yet anyway.

**Perhaps Mum and Dad do make sense,
because to do all the things I want to do when I grow up
I'll need to be clever and healthy.**